Franklin's Thanksgiving

With gratitude to all the farmers in the world – B.C.

Franklin

Franklin is a trademark of Kids Can Press Ltd.

Text © 2001 Contexx Inc.
Illustrations © 2001 Brenda Clark Illustrator Inc.

Story written by Sharon Jennings.

Interior illustrations prepared with the assistance of Shelley Southern.

Kids Can Press acknowledges the financial support of the Ontario Arts Council, the Canada Council for the Arts and the Government of Canada, through the BPIDP, for our publishing activity.

Published in Canada by   Published in the U.S. by
Kids Can Press Ltd.   Kids Can Press Ltd.
29 Birch Avenue   2250 Military Road
Toronto, ON M4V 1E2   Tonawanda, NY 14150

www.kidscanpress.com

Edited by Tara Walker

Printed in Hong Kong by Wing King Tong Company Limited

CM 01 0 9 8 7 6 5 4 3 2 1

Canadian Cataloguing in Publication Data

Jennings, Sharon
     Franklin's Thanksgiving

Based on characters created by Paulette Bourgeois and Brenda Clark.

ISBN 1-55074-798-3

I. Bourgeois, Paulette. II. Clark, Brenda. III. Title.

PS8569.E563F784 2001   jC813'.54   C00-933349-5
PZ7.J429877Frank 2001

Kids Can Press is a Nelvana company

Franklin's Thanksgiving

Story based on characters created by
Paulette Bourgeois and Brenda Clark
Illustrated by Brenda Clark

Kids Can Press

FRANKLIN liked everything about Thanksgiving. He liked eating pumpkin-fly pie and cranberry jelly. He liked making cornucopias and cornhusk dolls. But most of all, he liked having his Grandma and Grandpa come for dinner. It was the family tradition, and Franklin could hardly wait.

A week before Thanksgiving, a postcard arrived from Franklin's grandparents.

"Oh dear," sighed Franklin's mother. "Grandma and Grandpa can't make it back for the holiday."

"But they have to!" cried Franklin. "They're always here for Thanksgiving."

Franklin's mother gave him a hug. "There will still be the four of us," she said.

"It won't be the same," Franklin grumbled.

Over the next few days, Franklin was so busy that he didn't have much time to think about Grandma and Grandpa. He helped his mother pick apples and make applesauce. He helped his father dig up vegetables and store them in the cellar. Franklin and Bear helped Harriet and Beatrice pick berries and gather nuts.

In the gardens and orchards, forests and fields, everyone was bringing in the harvest.

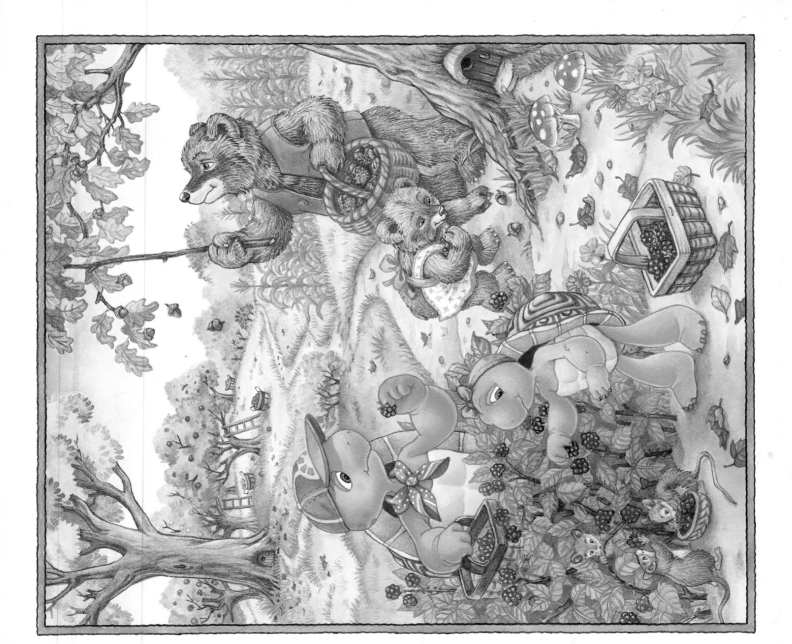

Franklin counted all the jars of jams and preserves. "I think this year was the most bountiful ever," announced his father. "We could feed the whole town!"

"I just wish we could feed Grandma and Grandpa," sighed Franklin.

His mother agreed. "We'll miss having company," she said.

At school, Franklin's class made a harvest quilt and learned how the early settlers celebrated Thanksgiving.

"What are you doing for Thanksgiving, Mr. Owl?" asked Franklin.

"I'll have dinner with my mother," he replied. "Our relatives can't visit this year."

"Ours neither," said Franklin.

Then he had an idea. He invited Mr. Owl and his mother for dinner.

"It's all right with my parents," Franklin explained. "They want company."

"Well, thank you, Franklin," said Mr. Owl. "We'd be delighted to come."

Franklin smiled. This would be a wonderful surprise for his parents.

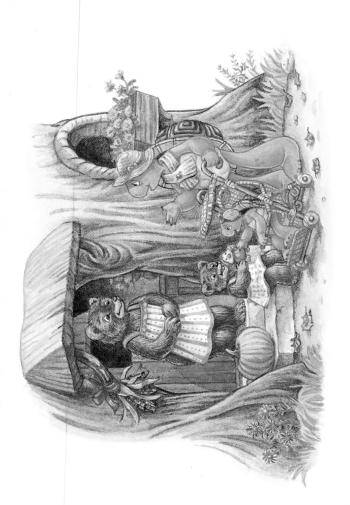

At home, Franklin's mother looked at the berry pies cooling on the windowsill.

She had an idea.

She walked over to Bear's house and invited the whole family for Thanksgiving.

"It will be a wonderful surprise for everyone," she explained.

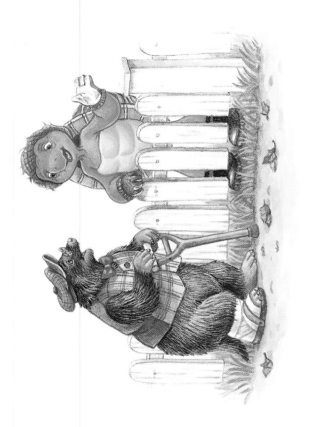

In the garden, Franklin's father waved to Mr. Mole. "Are you going to your sister's for Thanksgiving?" he asked.

"Not this year," replied Mr. Mole. "With my broken ankle, I can't go far."

Franklin's father had an idea. He invited Mr. Mole for dinner.

"It will be a wonderful surprise for everyone," he explained.

After school, Franklin went home with Moose.
That's when he had another idea.

It was the Moose family's first Thanksgiving in Woodland. Franklin invited them for dinner.

"It's all right with my parents," he explained.

"They want company."

"We'd be delighted," replied Mrs. Moose.

Franklin smiled. His surprise was getting bigger and bigger.

On Thanksgiving morning, Franklin got up early to help with dinner. He stirred soup and shucked corn. Then he set the table for nine.

Franklin's father counted the place settings. He shook his head and reset the table for five.

Franklin's mother looked at the table. She was puzzled, but she added three more place settings.

And everyone took turns peeking out the window, watching for the surprise guests.

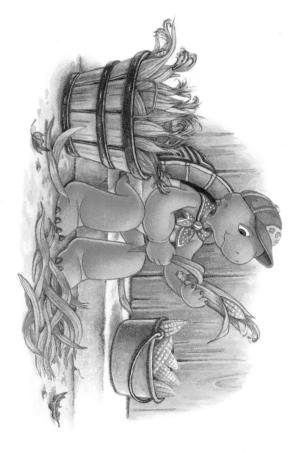

Mr. Owl and his mother were the first to arrive.

"Surprise!" Franklin shouted to his parents.

"This *is* a surprise!" they exclaimed.

Then Franklin saw the Bear family and Mr. Mole.

Now everyone was surprised.

All the guests crowded inside, holding platters and bowls heaped high with food.

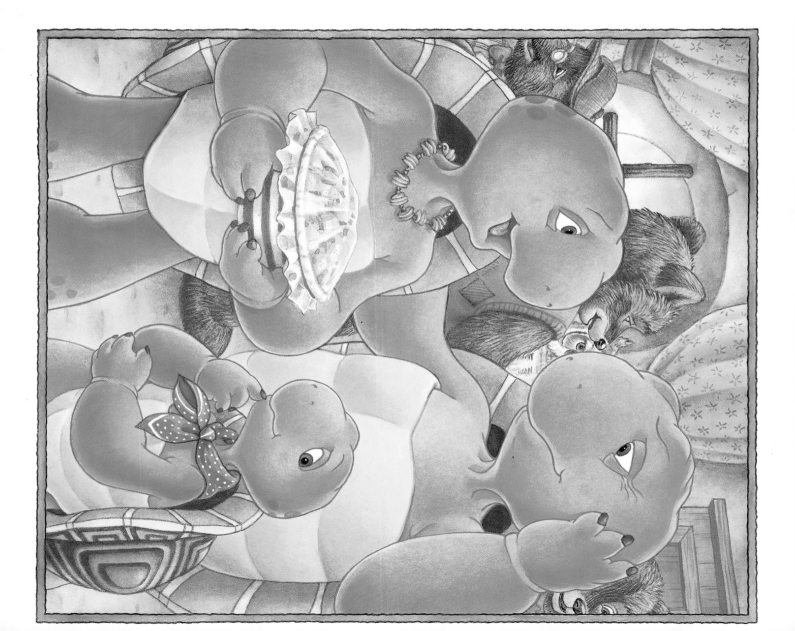

Franklin and his parents laughed and tried to explain what had happened.

"Well, we sure have plenty to eat," declared Franklin's mother. "We just don't have plenty of room."

Franklin knew they had a big problem.

The Moose family hadn't arrived yet.

Franklin looked around. There wasn't one bit of room inside. But outside ...

Suddenly, Franklin knew what to do.

Moose and his family arrived as all the others came out the door. Everyone carried food and dishes, tables and chairs.

"What's going on?" asked Moose.

"We're eating our Thanksgiving dinner in the field," answered Bear.

"Just like the early settlers," said Franklin.

It was a wonderful afternoon. Everyone ate lots of good food, and everyone said how thankful they were for good friends and family.

Franklin was thankful for three helpings of pumpkin-fly pie.

"I'm eating Grandma and Grandpa's share," he explained.

Soon the sun was setting and it was time to go home. "This was a wonderful day," said Franklin's mother. Franklin agreed. "Let's do it again next year!" he said. Everyone laughed and cheered.

Grandma and Grandpa phoned later that night, and Franklin told them all about the new Thanksgiving tradition. They promised that next year they wouldn't miss it for anything.

Franklin smiled. He might not get three helpings of pumpkin-fly pie next year, but he knew he'd still be thankful.